My "I AM" Song

With Love x.

Kelsie xo.

My "I AM" Song

Kelsie Josephs

Balboa Press books may be ordered through booksellers or by contacting:

Balboa Press
A Division of Hay House
1663 Liberty Drive
Bloomington, IN 47403
www.balboapress.com
1 (877) 407-4847

Because of the dynamic nature of the Internet, any web addresses or links contained in this book may have changed since publication and may no longer be valid. The views expressed in this work are solely those of the author and do not necessarily reflect the views of the publisher, and the publisher hereby disclaims any responsibility for them.

Any people depicted in stock imagery provided by Thinkstock are models, and such images are being used for illustrative purposes only.
Certain stock imagery © Thinkstock.

ISBN: 978-1-5043-7992-2 (sc)
ISBN: 978-1-5043-7993-9 (e)

Library of Congress Control Number: 2017906847

Print information available on the last page.

Balboa Press rev. date: 07/26/2017

BALBOA
PRESS
A DIVISION OF HAY HOUSE

Dedication

May this serve as a reminder to always see yourself
with **love** and **appreciation** for all that you are.

Choose to feel good about yourself each and
every day. You are **magnificent**!

When you say the words "*I AM*", remember to be kind.
Your day is a reflection of what is in your mind.

See yourself exactly how you want to be seen.

This is your reality; it isn't a dream.

When you're brushing your teeth or combing your hair,

look yourself in the eyes and love who is there.

Your thoughts are important
and so are your words,
so make sure that your "*I AM*s"
make you smile when they're heard!

I AM friendly, *I AM* honest and *I AM* loads of fun.
I AM happy, *I AM* humble, I shine as bright as the sun.
I AM loving, *I AM* caring and I have a huge heart.
I AM a positive person and boy, am I smart!

I AM enthusiastic and *I AM* grateful for all that I have.

I have a nice smile and a very contagious laugh.

I AM healthy, *I AM* creative and *I AM* very strong.

I AM kind, *I AM* gentle, this is my "*I AM*" song.

When I sing it I feel good, it makes my heart smile.
I know it's something I must do more than once in a while.
As I see myself exactly how I want to be seen,
so will the rest of the world, what a wonderful routine.

So *make sure* that you say your "*I AM*s",
but *make sure* that they're good!
Make sure that they're positive,
how you want to be understood.

They'll make you feel fuzzy.
They will fill you with light,
as you remind yourself of how special you are
in everyone's sight.

Positive Affirmations to Tell Yourself Every Day

I AM kind to everyone in my life!

I AM amazing!

I AM a generous person!

I AM so smart!

I AM beautiful from the inside, out!

I AM in perfect health!

I AM so blessed for all that I have!

I AM grateful for knowing how to shape my world!

I AM so much fun to be around!

I AM so full of light and love!

5 Steps to waking up HAPPY:

- Smile
- Give yourself a big hug – remember to start your day off LOVING you!
- Take **three** big deep breaths – this will make you feel great!
- *"Thank you, Thank you, Thank you"* – say this three times! As you say it, think about everything that you are grateful for.
- Set your **intention** for today: how do you want your day to unfold? What will you do to make *you* feel **happy?** – Maybe it's a walk. Maybe it's taking some extra time for yourself. Maybe, it's simply telling yourself that you will *be* kind and loving in all that you do today!

All is well. Everything is working out for your highest and greatest good. You are exactly where you need to be.

With all my Love and Light,

Kelsie

Kelsie Josephs is a writer of highly inspirational works for Thought Catalog along with many other articles rooted in positivity and love. Through her education degree and her passion for teaching children, she has made it her mission to awaken young minds to the powerful understanding that they are in control of their intentions, thoughts and in turn, lives. Kelsie has spread her love and wise words well beyond her hometown of Markham Ontario, Canada, reaching people everywhere.

CPSIA information can be obtained
at www.ICGtesting.com
Printed in the USA
LVHW01s1914030817
543752LV00011B/24/P